Jakers!
The Lost Shamrock

adapted by Alison Inches
images by Entara Ltd.

SIMON SPOTLIGHT
New York London Toronto Sydney

Hello, there. I'm Grandpa Piggley. Gather round and I'll tell you a story about when I was growing up down on Raloo Farm. *Jakers!* What fun we used to have . . .

Based on the TV series *Jakers! The Adventures of Piggley Winks* created by Entara Ltd.

SIMON SPOTLIGHT
An imprint of Simon & Schuster Children's Publishing Division
1230 Avenue of the Americas, New York, New York 10020

One day Piggley and his friends lost something important—something they had promised to take good care of, something that belonged to their teacher, Mr. Hornsby.

It happened on St. Patrick's Day—the day Piggley, Dannan, and Ferny were giving a report on Ireland.

Piggley had made a beautiful Irish harp, just like the ones on Irish coins.

Dannan had dressed like a leprechaun with a *shillelagh*, a walking stick, in her hand.

Ferny wore a pot-of-gold costume, complete with a cardboard rainbow hat.

"Piggley," said Dannan, "are you *sure* you brought everything for our report?"

"Of course I did!" said Piggley as he pulled the items from his book bag. "I brought our report, the flag of Ireland, the Irish coins, the Claddagh ring, and Mr. Hornsby's special shamrock."

"Uh-oh," said Piggley as he fished in his bag. "Mr. Hornsby's shamrock's gone missing!"

"I know it was in here!" said Piggley.
He put his book bag over his head to get a better look.

"This is really, *really* not good, Piggley!" cried Dannan as she paced back and forth. "Today's our report! What are we going to do?"

"I know!" said Ferny. "Papa says when you lose something, you need to think back to the last place you remember seeing it."

"Great idea!" said Piggley.

Piggley thought hard.

"The last time I saw the shamrock was yesterday when I was painting my harp. I put it in my pants pocket so it wouldn't get paint on it."

"Aha!" said Dannan. "Then it must be in your pants pocket."

Piggley searched his pockets.
"Oh, no!" said Piggley. "It's in my *other* pants pocket."

"Then go home and check them!" cried Dannan. "You can make it before the bell."

Piggley and Ferny raced to Piggley's house in record time.

Piggley found his pants and turned out the pockets.
"Nothing but a bunch of old hay!" he said.

"The hay!" cried Ferny. "It's from your barn—where we played circus yesterday! The shamrock fell out of your pocket when you were playing acrobat!"

"Jakers!" cried Piggley. "The shamrock must be in the barn—or worse, in the cow's stomach!"

"No!" cried Ferny. "Dannan found the shamrock when you went in to set the table. It's in the pocket of her sweater—the one she's wearing today!"

Piggley and Ferny raced back to school to tell Dannan.

"That's right! I *did* have the shamrock," said Dannan with a gasp. "I was going to give it to Piggley, but Grandma called me for supper so I gave it to Ferny!"

"Oh, Janey Mack!" cried Ferny. "How could I forget? I carried it to Piggley's house when Mr. Winks came out and offered me a ride home. I was so happy to get a lift that I put the shamrock in my coat pocket!"

Ferny searched his pockets. "Oh, no! It's not in here!"

"Now we're doomed for sure!" said Dannan.

Mr. Hornsby rang the school bell.

"Piggley! Dannan! Ferny! Your report is next," said Mr. Hornsby.

The gloomy friends plodded to the front of the room.

"Mr. Hornsby," said Dannan, "we have a bit of bad news."
But before they had a chance to tell him, Don Toro walked into the classroom.

"Please pardon me for interrupting your class," said Don Toro. "But Fernando forgot his lunch this morning."

Ferny swiveled in his pot-of-gold suit. "Now I remember!" he said. "Papa found the shamrock in my coat last night and put it in my lunch so I wouldn't forget it!"

"You mean to say you *lost* my special shamrock?" said Mr. Hornsby. "The one I told you to take good care of?"

"Yes, sir," said Ferny. "But we all tried to remember where we last saw it—just like Papa taught me to do."

"Well, now, that's very good advice," said Mr. Hornsby. "And it certainly worked because my shamrock is no longer lost."

"Not lost at all!" said Piggley.

And with a sigh of relief they began their report on Ireland.

Happy St. Patrick's Day!